For my family: Chris, Manny, Mary, Randy, and my basketball experts Keith, Jeff, and Matt.

-KAGB

I would like to dedicate this book to my late Father, {David Colin Llewelyn Gray} who passed away when I was fifteen years old. He Always encouraged me to follow my heart, and pursue my goals. And never pressured me into being anything but myself.

-HG

MacLaren-Cochrane Publishing

Text © 2017 Kimberly A. Gordon Biddle

Cover and Interior Art © 2017 Heath Gray

LaDonna Plays Hoops

MacLaren-Cochrane Publishing
620 Buchanan Way, Folsom, CA 95630

Library of Congress Control Number: 2017910815

First Edition

ISBN
Hardcover: 978-1-365-86147-5
Softcover: 978-1-365-86151-2

For orders, visit
www.maclaren-cochranepublishing.com
www.facebook.com/maclaren-cochranepublishing

LaDonna Plays Hoops

By Kimberly A. Gordon Biddle

Illustrated by Heath Gray

"I wonder what Grandma looks like now? Maybe she has more grey hair and wrinkles, Freddy," I say to my lime green pet frog. "Daddy, when will we get there? I want to play with Cousin Felicia."

"We'll be there soon, Honey," my daddy says. "Felicia's brother, Tyrone, will be there, too."

"Tyrone, the family hoops star, but maybe not for long," I state. I remember playing Tyrone two years ago before summer basketball camp. Fifty free throw shots, with a basket too tall for me. Tyrone proved he was better. He laughed when he won. He teased me, but at five years old I felt the stinging shame of missing shots and losing.

"Now, LaDonna, it's been two years since you played Tyrone. He won't beat you as bad. Besides, playing him will help you get better," Daddy says. The car pulls up to an old house with peeling paint. Grandma is in the doorway with silvery, sunlit hair and smooth skin.

"Well, it's my little tomboy in a frilly, pink dress with blue leggings," Grandma says, waving in the doorway. "I haven't seen you in awhile; you must've grown two feet!" Grandma hugs me tightly.

"Hi, Grandma. Is Felicia here?" I say.

"Why yes, and your other cousins," Grandma states. "They're all out back. Why don't you and Freddy go join them? Tyrone is in the driveway with your uncles playing basketball."

I frown and hesitate.
"He's been waiting," says Grandma.

Running to the back yard with Freddy, I see Felicia, Veronica, and Sharlene playing double dutch. My older cousins Amber and Charles are playing Bid Whist on Grandma's patio table.

"Hello," I say.

"It's LaDonna and Freddy!" everyone says. My pet frog is a big part of the family. Felicia, Veronica, and Sharlene stop playing double dutch and run over to touch Freddy's cold and slimy skin. They look at each other and giggle.

"I haven't played double dutch in a long time. Can I play?" I ask.

"I'll watch Freddy for you," says my cousin Veronica.

Felicia, Sharlene, and I begin playing double dutch. Just then a loud "Yeah" comes from the driveway. Tyrone comes running and yells, "We won!"

I trip over the double dutch rope and skin my knee. The blood seeps through my blue leggings and the pain is prickly.

Amber and Charles stop playing cards and get a cold, wet cloth to wipe and bandage my knee. I walk around and soon it feels better.

Then Tyrone says, while dribbling the ball, "Hey, LaDonna, are you okay? Do you want to play a game of hoops with me?"
I knew this moment was coming. Tyrone towers over me. All eyes turn to look at me and I wonder if I can beat the family hoops star. Then I think of two years ago.

"I just might go play basketball," I say. "Veronica, please keep an eye on Freddy."

I run to the driveway in my dress, leggings, and bandages and shout, "One-on-one, first to ten, two-point spread!"

"Look, Half Pint, I'll play you a game of PIG," says Tyrone.

"Stop calling me Half Pint! I've grown. I want to play one-on-one" I state.

"OK, Cuz," says Tyrone, "You do know that I play AAU league ball now, right?"

"Let's flip for first," I say
"No, Cuz, you go first. This shouldn't take too long," smirks Tyrone.

"Even with my hurt leg, I can beat you," I boast. But, I wonder if I can do this?

"LaDonna, it's not about winning. It's how you play the game. Just do your best," Daddy says.

My entire family moves to the driveway,
even Veronica with Freddy.

"Game on," Tyrone exclaims and bounces the ball to me. I dribble past him and make a layup. The hoop doesn't seem as tall as last time. Another bounce to me and I score two more points in the paint. 4-0.

Next, Tyrone bounces the ball high. I run, catch it, and launch a three. "Tres Up!" 7-0.

My leg hurts and the bandage falls. Time out! Now I clean, wipe, and bandage my own knee.

"LaDonna, don't stop now," Tyrone says.

"I'm not quitting, Cuz. I just need 3 more points," I say.

"Watch this," Tyrone smiles.

Tyrone bounces another high one. I run, get it, shoot the three and miss. It's Tyrone's ball. I bounce it; he catches it and releases a three.
     "Sweet, tres up," he says.

And then Tyrone makes 2 three-pointers in a row. 7-9. Time out! My knee hurts. I walk around again.

"Give up now, Cuz?" Tyrone asks.

"No, the game's to 10. I haven't beaten you yet," I say.

"OK, LaDonna," Tyrone smirks.

I bounce the ball. Tyrone brings it in for a layup. I jump and block the ball.

"Foul!" Tyrone exclaims.

"No foul!" Daddy yells with other family members.

Tyrone bounces the ball hard and high and rushes towards me.
I catch and release it, making it rain. Tres up! 10-9.

"You need another point," Tyrone exclaims and bounces the ball. I catch it and fake; he goes for the fake. I crossover, dribble into the lane, and elevate for a jump shot. 12-9.

"I won. I really won!" I exclaim.

"I beat you so bad last time that I just let you win. I want a rematch!" Tyrone exclaims.

I beam with a smile, "Maybe in two years, because I'm the family hoops star now! But don't worry, Cuz, you'll always have front row seats to my games!

Kimberly Gordon Biddle
Author

Kimberly A. Gordon Biddle is a lover of books. Her nose was always in a book, when she was younger. She still loves to read, when she gets the chance, and she also loves to write. She has co-authored a textbook on early childhood education and is under contract to co-author one about child development careers. "LaDonna Plays Hoops" is her first book of fiction. This picture book was born in the 1980's and has grown and matured. Seeing the book come to life is a realized dream for Kimberly. For her day job, she is a professor of child development. Kimberly is also a member of the Society for Children's Book Writers and Illustrators (SCBWI). She is also a loving wife to her husband and a loving mother to her son. She currently lives in the Nor Cal area of California. She has a BA in Psychology and Music and a PhD in Child and Adolescent Development.

Heath Gray
Illustrator

Heath {James} Gray was born in West Auckland, New Zealand. Heath has had a passion for illustration from the time he could pick up a pencil. He started out as a sign writer from the age of fifteen. Attended a graphic design course at Auckland University of Technology, Heath worked as a 2d character animator for eight years, where he trained under a Disney animator, {John Ewing.} Here he worked on television shows for Disney, and Warner Bros. Heath also worked on many New Zealand TV series, and commercials. {And directed two of these TV commercials.} Heath has dedicated his life to illustration, and specializes in children's book, and cartoon illustrations. There is nothing else Heath would rather do than illustration, except perhaps travel the world in a Hot air balloon.

Heath is also the illustrator of *Tilly the Turtle* released in 2017.

To view more of Heath Gray's illustration work, Feel free to go to Deviant Art, where Heath Gray also goes under the alias
Name, verbarlin.
http://www.deviantart.com/browse/all/?section=&global=1&q=verbarlin

CPSIA information can be obtained
at www.ICGtesting.com
Printed in the USA
BVIC01n1642201017
497896BV00007B/10